Kenan Furlong is an Irish writer. Originally from Wexford, he now lives in Dublin with his family.

The author's proceeds from the sale of this book will be donated to the Irish Cancer Society.

Kenan Furlong

HOCKER ALLEY

AUSTIN MACAULEY PUBLISHERS™

LONDON · CAMBRIDGE · NEW YORK · SHARJAH

A CIP catalogue record for this title is available from the British Library.

ISBN 9781398449169 (Paperback)
ISBN 9781398449176 (ePub e-book)

www.austinmacauley.com

First Published 2022
Austin Macauley Publishers Ltd®
1 Canada Square
Canary Wharf
London
E14 5AA

I was lucky to be taught English by two very capable teachers: Eddie Cassidy and Victor Martin of St Peter's College, Wexford. I was encouraged to read by supportive, loving parents, Ronan and Colette.

If I had listened more to all of their astute guidance, then I would never have found myself, as a post-graduate law student, approaching my former school principal and author/poet, Philip Quirke, to ask him to teach me how to write. It speaks volumes about Philip's character that he so readily agreed to help someone who had already been given every opportunity to learn. His fee for hours of one-on-one tuition with an undeserving student? A packet of cigarettes.

This book would not have been written without Philip. More importantly, he also taught me to enjoy writing it.

Philip's wife, the author/poet, Margaret Galvin, also played a key role in reviewing initial drafts and stimulating ideas when I reached an impasse. This book would not have been published without her.

Thanks to my brother, Ronan, my sister, Leah, and the aforementioned Colette for their helpful feedback on various drafts.

Thanks also to my good friend, Daniel Scanlon, for reminding me once upon a time that inspiration was just a 'rice paper' away.

I am grateful also to my former business partners and mentors, Eoin MacNeill and Liam Kennedy of A&L Goodbody, for teaching me how, when it comes to writing, 'less is more'.

I should also give a 'shoutout' to the late, great Charles Bukowski. Reading his work was the first time it occurred to me that I could try this writing lark.

Finally, thanks to my wife, Sinéad; and my children, Milo and Martha, for their patience and support.

*"...Time held me green and dying
Though I sang in my chains like the sea."*
Dylan Thomas, *Fern Hill*

Wexford in the 1980s was a proud county synonymous with a bloody, glorious, and, ultimately, suppressed rebellion nearly two-hundred years earlier, in 1798. Then, against all odds and using vastly inferior weaponry, the Wexford battalion of the United Irishmen had won famous and heroic victories at Oulart, Enniscorthy and Wexford town. It took the introduction of twenty-thousand extra British troops to finally defeat the rebels at the Battle of Vinegar Hill.

The rebellion remained a great source of pride in the county. The United Irishmen had not thrown off the shackles of British rule but their *'terribly beautiful'* defeat had inspired others to do so, for better or worse. Rebel songs like *'the Boys of Wexford'*, *'Kelly the Boy from Killane'* and *'Boolavogue'* were sung with feeling in every school.

*****

In the autumn of 1980, a six-year-old Declan 'Deccy' Tennant started playing football for Oulart United in the Wexford District Football League. For the next eight years, he was one of the best footballers in the County and certainly the most talented.

Tennant looked and played like no one else and he revelled in his uniqueness. He wore his unruly fringe a little too long and was constantly brushing it to one side. His socks were permanently halfway down his calves. He strutted around like a peacock, demanding possession when he didn't have the ball. He was a sight to behold when he did.

Oulart United played in the comfortable environs of the third division. This allowed Tennant the time and space to display the full repertoire of skills he honed playing street football on his council estate. Nutmegs, drag-backs, double drag-backs, bicycle-kicks; you name it, he did it. He glided across the pitch like a downhill skier, jinking impetuously between defenders. He had a wand of a left foot that allowed him to remain in total control of the ball. If he had been born in Manchester in the mid-eighties (and had a lot less acne) then you would never have heard of David Beckham.

Tennant had a simple, trademark celebration pose when he scored. He would raise both his arms straight out to the side, like an aeroplane, and glide away from the goal. I don't know where he got it but it looked good.

*****

I had the good fortune to be Tennant's midfield partner with Oulart United for most of his underage football. I had none of his skill but was pretty dogged and enjoyed the defensive side of the game. I once heard our coach comment about me that *'he isn't blessed with talent but if a plastic bag blows across the pitch, he tackles it'*.

My defensive instincts were the perfect foil for Tennant's creative genius. Our team had a very simple but effective game plan: Plan A was *'give the ball to Tennant'*, Plan B was *'don't forget Plan A'*. I was happy to follow those instructions. I used to joke that Tennant and I were *'the best midfield pairing in Wexford'*; for a while, Tennant was so good that he and *any* other player in Wexford would arguably have been the best midfield pairing in the county.

*****

Tennant's home life was less idyllic. He was raised by a single mum, Josie, who was *'fond of the jar'*. No one spoke of his dad. It was as if he didn't have one.

Josie's favourite drink was a free one. However, now in her mid-forties but looking much older, the days of persuading a male companion in the Oulart Tavern to buy her a few drinks were long gone.

Her meagre dole payment every Thursday was barely enough for the groceries, her fags, and a bottle of Bushmills. When a choice had to be made between paying utility bills and an excursion to the Oulart Tavern, the bills were sometimes allowed to mount up until the gas cooker gasped to a dismal halt.

She had long given up on her appearance and tended to postpone getting her hair done until she *'could afford it'*. She raked her thin smoke-stained fingers through straw-yellow, half-grey hair on days when she could not find her comb. On signing-on days, she roused herself out of her pyjamas and pulled on a sagging tracksuit and a frayed denim jacket for the trip to the dole office.

The booze affected her kidneys as much as it affected her speech. On return trips from the Oulart Tavern, they said that *'you would smell her before you'd see her'*.

*****

It had not always been that way. In fact, for most of Tennant's life, Josie had been a sober and doting mother.

Josie's pregnancy was unexpected and unwanted. However, once she came to terms with being pregnant, she looked forward to having a child. The house the council allocated to her was adequate but she was new to the estate. She was not good on her own and thought a child would turn the house into a home.

She devoured Tennant with her fierce maternal love. So what if she lived from hand to mouth or if her no-good relatives ignored her? She gave Tennant the one commodity that she had in abundance and that all children need: time. She spent every waking moment with him. They developed a mutual affinity for Abba music, which they sometimes sang together as she paused in her sloppy efforts to wash the floor. She would lift him up into her arms to share the occasional waltz to the strains of their favourite song, *'Fernando'*. Her improvised favourite line – *'There was something in the air that night, the stars were bright, Oh Deccyyyy'* – never failed to prompt a smile from both of them as she whisked him around the kitchen.

She took him everywhere: to the shops, the dole office, and, on a daily basis, to the playground in Redmond Park. She was naturally shy and found it hard to talk to people. However, Tennant drew people to her and that was a gift. She enjoyed talking to them about his sleeping routines, how big he was getting, and whether Santa was coming. The stigma which had attached to her pregnancy and the 'mystery father' dissolved as she glowed.

*****

Josie's birthday presents to Tennant were modest, frequently from charity shops. He didn't care. He loved train sets, even shabby ones with the odd track missing. He amassed quite a collection in his bedroom.

Tennant's fifth birthday was to be his best. Josie, leafing through a magazine in a newsagent as she escaped the rain, had hit on a great idea. At 9 am on the big day, she dragged Tennant out of his bed to make the early train from Wexford to Dublin. From there they got another train to Malahide, a picturesque seaside village on the north coast of Dublin and home to the resplendent Malahide castle.

Tennant spent the entire journey gazing out at the stunning Leinster coastline and wandering excitedly up and down the carriages. It was his first time on a train. Josie's futile attempts to read a discarded magazine were interrupted by Tennant's awestruck commentary on the journey:

"Ma, we're in a tunnel!"
"Ma, we're in another tunnel!"
"Ma, they sell crisps on this train!"
"Ma, did you hear? That man said we're arriving in Wicklow soon."

Josie greeted each announcement as if it was a shared discovery.

Tennant assumed the train journey was his birthday present. However, Josie had something special up her sleeve at the end of the line.

They got off the train at Malahide, directly opposite the grand, tree-lined entrance to Malahide castle.

"Where are we going, ma?"
"You'll see," Josie replied, beaming.

Tennant's eyes darted left and right as he walked up the avenue, holding his mother's hand. He saw his first-ever cricket match unfold on the manicured lawn to the right. He marvelled at the speed of the bowlers and the players' brilliant whites. Then, as he neared the castle, he noticed the *'Fry Model Railway'* sign outside a white building with a thatched roof. Before Josie could contain him, he let go of her hand and was sprinting to the entrance, turning back every few metres to beckon her on. She did her best to catch up, laughing, out of breath and almost as excited as him.

The Fry Model Railway was Ireland's largest model railway, about the size of a tennis court. Tennant was in heaven. For the next hour, he dashed excitedly from one part to another, following the trains through the mountain tunnels, past the windmills, along the bridges and over the rivers. It was better than *'Willy Wonka's chocolate factory'*.

To cap it all, Josie had cut down on her smokes for the previous fortnight so that she had enough to buy him a toy train from the gift shop. Tennant spent forty-five minutes surveying every train on the shelves. How could he possibly choose? He tormented the shop assistant with questions about each one as he mulled over his options. Finally, he settled on a bright red 'Malahide Steamer'. It would take a pride of place in his collection at home. Josie thanked and apologised to the assistant as she handed over the cash.

The June sun shone through the window of their carriage on the train home. Tennant had the Malahide Steamer in one hand and a packet of Tayto crisps, which he shared with Josie, in the other. He was happy. The posh pensioner reading his newspaper opposite them could not help but be distracted by Tennant's incessant chatter to Josie about all the trains he had seen as if she had not been there herself. He folded his newspaper as he was about to disembark and remarked:

"Well, it sounds like you had a great birthday. Aren't you a lucky boy?"

And he was.

For the next five years, whenever Tennant was sick or woke up with a nightmare, Josie would lie beside him and recall their trip to Malahide. It was a memory that would never fade. For either of them.

*****

Tennant became more independent as adolescence arrived. There was no shortage of kids on his estate who shared his lack of enthusiasm for homework. His sublime footballing skills drew others of all ages to him. They played endless games on the streets as the light faded in the evenings. Josie would occasionally watch with pride from her bedroom window, making sure to remain unseen. Tennant was in his element out there.

Coincidence or not, it was around that time she started drinking excessively, with a bottle of whiskey a permanent fixture on her bedside locker. Tennant spent less time at home and she had more time on her hands. Bushmills and daytime television helped it pass.

Her bond with Tennant was still strong though. On Sunday nights they watched *Dallas* together on the couch, pretending for the others' sake that they enjoyed it more than they did. It was the one night of the week that Josie never visited the Oulart Tavern.

*****

My house was less than a mile from Tennant's. That quirk of geography dictated that he and I went to the same primary and secondary schools and played for the same football team. However, our futures looked very different from the beginning.

I was from a comfortable middle-class, happy home. I had a 'mum', not a 'ma', and mine collected me in her car after school. He walked to/from both school and football training from his council estate. He had his own house keys. Sometimes Josie was there when he got home, sometimes she wasn't. By the time we went to secondary school, he spent more time looking after her than she did for him.

Off the pitch, he inherited his mother's natural shyness and didn't say much. Football was the only language he was articulate in.

The social chasm between us was such that we were never destined to be best mates. Still, you can't play that many matches with someone without getting to know them in some way. We got on pretty well for two kids who had little in common except Oulart United.

St Enda's Boys' School had some great teachers. However, it was a tough school where there was a constant undercurrent of violence. You were as likely to catch a beating in the classroom as in the yard. *'Squealing'* (telling tales) was a cardinal sin and was typically met with immediate ostracization.

In one corner of the yard, concrete steps lead down to a small alley adjoining a boiler room, known as *'Hocker Alley'*. The rules of entry were as simple as they were disgusting: everyone was allowed to '*hock*' (spit) on a kid who had the misfortune to be thrust down there. It was like being suddenly caught in a cascade of snot and saliva. It was even worse in winter when a lot of kids had colds and could hock *'greeners'* that would stick to the wall if they missed the target. Bullies stood guard near the top of the steps. Those pushed in had to fight their way out.

'Nuts' Roche was one of Hocker Alley's most menacing centurions and one of the hardest lads in St Enda's. His moniker came from his red-hot temper and violent disposition; he'd had to be dragged off a few of those misfortunate enough to trade blows with him long after they were unable to defend themselves. He didn't know or care when they'd had enough.

In Tennant's second year at St. Ends, Nuts got into an altercation with Tennant during a lunchtime football match. He didn't like Tennant dribbling nonchalantly past him with the ball. After the match was over and the ref had returned to the staff room, he tried to push Tennant into Hocker Alley. Tennant resisted and a fight broke out.

Everyone expected it to end abruptly with Tennant seeing stars. However, Tennant hadn't read the script. He connected with a couple of early haymakers which stunned Nuts. Nuts recovered quickly though and was well on top by the time a teacher, Pat Treacy, arrived to break it up. By then, Tennant had taken a proper pounding. Blood poured from his nose into his mouth. He gave a bloody smile and blew kisses to the baying crowd as Mr Treacy escorted himself and Nuts to the principal's office.

Tennant had lost the fight but had taken his beating well. That kind of toughness had real currency in St Enda's. His stock has risen in defeat.

Both boys were suspended and informed that their parents were being telephoned to collect them from school. Nuts' mother was there, scowling, with a face like a smacked arse, within half an hour, leaving Tennant sitting on his own outside the principal's office.

*****

Hours later, I got sent from class on an errand to the office. Tennant was still sitting there. As I approached, I stumbled on a scene, which would define my relationship with him.

Mrs McGrath, the secretary, was a kind woman. A mother herself, she was full of empathy when she slowly explained to Tennant that she had been unable to contact Josie. She promised to keep trying. Tennant, unaware of my arrival, burst into a stuttering, hopeless sob. I couldn't understand how he could take all Nuts had given him without even a whimper and then disintegrate on hearing Mrs McGrath's update. Maybe he knew where Josie was or maybe it was because he didn't. Mrs McGrath seemed to understand and did her best to comfort him.

I wished I wasn't there. I turned around and began to walk away slowly, hoping he wouldn't see me. When I looked back Tennant had his head in his hands but caught my eye through a gap in his fingers. We both knew that if I blabbed then his hard-earned reputation would be lost.

That was never going to happen. I gave him a wink and mimicked his goal celebration pose, holding out my arms to the side like aeroplane wings, as I walked away. I hoped he would see it as a gesture of solidarity and know that I wouldn't breathe a word.

Tennant returned to school the following week. By then he had figured out that his secret was safe with me.

That weekend, I scored a rare and insignificant goal for Oulart United. Before I knew it, I felt someone jump up on my back and scream *'Go on ye boy ye'*. It was Tennant's way of saying thanks.

*****

Clem Roche was the coach of the Wexford under-sixteen county football team and a really decent sort. By day he was a postman. However, that job description did not come close to describing the service he provided, particularly to isolated, elderly members of his community. He knew that for some he was the only person they might speak with that day. They timed the tending of their tiny front gardens to coincide with his mail run. To them he was part post man, part social worker and part weatherman. A man of rare charm, he never tired of exchanging the same cheerful pleasantries a dozen times per morning with those who wanted or needed a quick word:

'No mail today, Mary. You'll have to tell Sean Connery that you're not happy with the silent treatment you're getting from him'

'Well, George. When are you having that hip operation? I hear Jack Charlton is hoping you'll be fit in time for the World Cup.'

'Morning, Angela. Don't forget that the clocks move forward tonight. There'll be a grand stretch in the evening tomorrow.'

Against his better judgment (and his employer's guidelines), he also found it impossible to resist doing the odd small favour for those who had no one else to ask:

'Clem, while you're here, would you mind just changing that light bulb for me? My balance is not great these days.

'Of course, I wouldn't mind, Martin, but only if you promise not to sue me if I electrocute you…'

An animal lover, he was nearly as popular with the collection of mutts he passed, who he sometimes treated to the remains of his breakfast sausages from a white hanky in his pockets.

His animal magnetism did not end there, either. Tanned and fit, he occasionally, and embarrassingly, had to spurn the advances of certain of Wexford's more desperate housewives who wanted him to do more than change their light bulb.

They were wasting their time. He married his childhood sweetheart, Marie, when they were nineteen and had now been together for over twenty-five years. They were husband and wife, best friends and had been through a lot. In particular, they had spent over ten years being referred from one doctor to another as their increasingly desperate attempts to start a family faltered. Infertility had been a tortuous journey of daily prayers, invasive treatment, anxious waiting rooms, and dashed hopes. Clem Roche privately dreaded administering the daily hormone injections deep into Marie's thigh as she grimaced in pain. However, nothing hurt more than the insensitive questions in social settings about the absent children they were trying so desperately to have.

The end came eventually in a fertility clinic on Harley Street, London. Marie stared blankly out the window as the Indian consultant broke the now familiar news. She had too much pride to cry in his office. However, she dissolved on Clem Roche's shoulder as soon as they re-emerged into the Harley Street air.

It was over and they knew it. However, here was no relief, only dejection. There would always be someone missing from their lives.

They left London physically, emotionally, and financially drained. They promised each other on the deck of the ferry back from Wales that they would spend the rest of their lives focusing on each other and their beloved pets. Firmly holding each other's hand as the Wexford coastline reappeared; they agreed that *'want what you have'* would become their new motto.

*****

Clem Roche and Marie went on a holiday to Lanzarote around the same time as Tennant returned to St Enda's from his suspension. During a romantic walk on the seafront, Clem Roche noticed that an English pub was showing a match involving his beloved Liverpool team that night. He took a mental note to 'stretch his legs' again later, just in time for the 8 pm kick-off.

His plan worked. Ordering a pint at the bar, he started chatting with a scouser called Andy Clarke, who was there on a similar pilgrimage. It turned out that Clarke, whose mother was Irish, was coach to the under sixteen football team for Queens Park Rangers and a fellow Liverpool fan.

QPR's first team played in the First Division of the English Football League. Clarke's under sixteen team were due to play a tournament in Dublin in July, against a handful of the best schoolboy teams from Ireland. It was partly a chance to sharpen their skills and partly a scouting mission for Irish talent.

Clem Roche saw this as his opportunity. He explained that his Wexford under sixteen team had reached the semi-finals of the All-Ireland tournament last year and was a match for the teams that Clarke's QPR team would play in the Dublin tournament. Wexford was only *'down the road'* (ahem, eighty-six miles) from Dublin. The Wexford team would be delighted to give the QPR lads a warm-up game before the tournament if Clarke was interested.

Three pints and a stirring Liverpool win later, he and Clarke shook on it and exchanged telephone numbers.

The cream of English football was coming to Wexford.

Tennant was the only Oulart United player named in the Wexford Squad of sixteen to play QPR. He didn't make the starting eleven though and was instead named as one of five substitutes.

He was fifteen now and had lost none of his skill. However, his haphazard diet usually consisted of coco pops and chips. He had also started pilfering Josie's fags on the not infrequent occasions when she was too drunk to notice. He despised running that was not in pursuit of a football. His increasing lack of athleticism meant his flashes of brilliance were more sporadic and usually confined to the first thirty minutes of matches.

Some felt that he was lucky to even make it into the squad. He was well on his way to becoming a lad with a great future behind him.

*****

Tennant's place in the squad for the QPR match was big news on his estate. His mates wondered if he would get a chance to show the QPR lads the repertoire of tricks he had honed with them.

Josie had not been to one of his games since he started to be slagged by the lads about her escorting him to matches. This game, however, was an important one and a day he might never forget. She knew that she should be there but didn't want to go. She had heard that her drinking habits were talked about by the town gossips. She knew very little about football. The thought of attending the match on her own made her heart pelt with nervousness. *'Who would she talk to? What would she wear? What if someone made fun of her?'*

Nonetheless, she genuinely intended to attend the game as she left their house on match day. Unfortunately, her plan also involved a pit stop in the Oulart Tavern for a quick shot of Dutch courage to help with her social skills.

The reasons for not attending the game become more and more compelling with every drop she swallowed. *'Would he be nervous if he saw her? Would he feel bad if he didn't play? What would she say to him after the match?'*

*****

Conditions on match day were perfect. East End United's pitch was bathed in brilliant sunshine. A light breeze blew invigorating fresh sea air across the turf.

There must have been five hundred spectators on the sideline, including me. Also in attendance was Mick 'Scoop' Murphy from the *Wexford Times.* Murphy had a gut on him like a heavily pregnant woman. Locals joked beneath their breath that his nickname was derived, not from his journalistic prowess, but from his fondness for ice cream.

It was not every day that a club from England's First Division came to play in Wexford. Everyone agreed that Clem Roche had pulled a masterstroke in luring such illustrious opposition.

A frisson of excitement swept through the ground when QPR's team bus, resplendent in their signature blue and white stripes, pulled in, their proud club-crest on the front.

QPR's players descended, as if in slow motion, their shiny blue and white tracksuits glistening in the sun. Square jawed and athletic, with clear skin, they looked like some form of a master race.

The Wexford players leaned against a wall, their battered gear bags slung over their shoulders, like a pack of mongrels watching Crufts. Under strict instructions to be there on time, they had been waiting anxiously for half an hour that felt like ages. They had chewed gum, smoked fags, scratched their balls, burst their yellowheads and speculated about whether QPR would actually show up. It was the first time that some of them had seen a black person. They looked fast.

Drawn mostly from the tougher parts of the county, one of the Wexford players, midfielder Damian 'Demo' Larkin, had spent the morning robbing lawn mowers and selling them for hash, his two accomplices now among the spectators. The Wexford players trudged over to their makeshift changing room, trying to control the butterflies in their stomach. All bar one of them was now focused on the game ahead. Demo Larkin's focus, however, was elsewhere. He glanced over at his two friends in their crowd and wondered if QPR would remember to lock the bus…

Clem Roche was intoxicated by seeing his vision realised. It felt like he was living a movie. After greeting Andy Clarke, he spent five minutes obsequiously thanking him again for bringing their team over and insisting the Wexford lads would play a good, fair game.

*****

Wexford's deferential approach continued after kick-off. They were 0–1 down within minutes.

Wexford's befreckled red-haired goalkeeper, Thomas 'Spud' Flood, was understandably nervous. It was the first time he had played in front of a crowd like that. He parried a QPR cross that he would normally catch into the path of a QPR striker, who casually stroked it into the net. Too easy. Spud swore loudly in exasperation. Everyone was embarrassed. The air of anticipation that greeted the kick-off evaporated instantly.

The second goal arrived shortly before halftime and was the least that QPR deserved. An intricate passing move between QPR's midfield and strikers culminated in a lovely finish by the same striker who scored the first goal. 0–2.

The QPR players joked as they strolled off at halftime. The Wexford lads bickered among themselves; the ship was sinking fast with their family and friends there to witness it. It was everybody else's fault.

Clem Roche did his best to raise their spirits. It was no use. They had lost the match before a ball was kicked when they were entranced by the QPR regalia.

*****

The second half started in near silence. The procession continued.

QPR hit the crossbar twice in the first fifteen minutes. Then a long-range shot from a QPR midfielder flew into the top corner of Wexford's net. 0–3.

The crowd on the side-line became uneasy.

"This isn't doing anyone any good," they began to mutter darkly.

Scoop Murphy had come to the game directly from a funeral he was covering. He was finding the eulogy helpful as he began to contemplate the most benign match report he could possibly write about such a one-sided game. The Wexford lads had *'fought the good fight'* and *'kept going until the end'* he mused.

The entire QPR team jogged to join their midfielder in executing an elaborate pre-rehearsed dance routine goal celebration. As they did, one of Wexford's strikers approached Clem Roche on the side-line to tell him that he had pulled his hamstring and could not continue.

Wexford were 3–0 down. Their heads had dropped. They had already used all three substitutes allowed and were therefore about to be reduced from eleven to ten men. There were still twenty-five minutes left. If it was a boxing match the ref would have stopped it to avoid Wexford enduring further and unnecessary punishment.

No one could have anticipated what was about to happen.

*****

Andy Clarke saw Wexford's striker limping off. He said to Clem Roche:

"Why don't you stick on another sub? Then I could give another one of my lads a run too."

It was the gesture of a true sportsman aimed at keeping the game remotely competitive; QPR would only use two of their allotted three substitutes that day. Clem Roche knew it was an offer he could not afford to turn down.

"*Thanks,*" he said, with a grateful, knowing nod to his counterpart.

Wexford had two subs left: Mark 'Chopper' Ryan, an uncompromising defender known for his reckless tackling, and Tennant, a striker. Both had earlier seen Wexford's third, and final permitted substitute entering the fray and therefore assumed they would not be playing.

Clem Roche was tempted to put Chopper Ryan on to try and stem the bleeding. However, he realised that what the Wexford team needed more than anything else was a goal so they could take something positive from the day; 1–4 would be better than 0–3. There was just one problem: Chopper stood beside him but there was no sign of Tennant.

"Where the hell is Deccy Tennant?" he said to Chopper, exasperated.

"I think he's having a piss. I'll go get him," replied Chopper.

Tennant wasn't pissing. He was having a sneaky fag behind the Portakabin that served as Wexford's dressing room.

Chopper found him.

"Hey, Marlboro Man, you're on!"

Tennant took a drag of his dwindling fag and, exhaling slowly, said:

"You need to work on your maths, mate. We've already used our three subs."

"Their manager is letting us use <u>all</u> our subs. I might be on me self soon…"

Tennant stubbed out his fag on the wall of the Portakabin and sauntered over to the side-line. He casually removed his Wexford training top like a geriatric gingerly taking off his pyjamas and inserted into his socks the undersized shin guards he had used since under twelve days.

Clem Roche turned to offer him the usual substitute's instructions. However, staring at Tennant for a moment, he paused, and then simply said:

"Deccy, you're on."

Some birds aren't meant to be caged.

He then shouted at the ref for permission to introduce Tennant into the fray.

*****

Tennant's entrance went all but unnoticed, coinciding with Wexford's kick-off after the third goal. He jogged out onto the pitch wearing number fourteen, stopping after a few yards to bend down, touch the grass with his right hand and then bless himself. It was oddly religious behaviour for a lad that had not darkened the door of a church since his communion eight years ago. However, he had seen the Brazilian footballers observe the same ritual during the last World Cup and thought it looked pretty cool. He was right.

Tennant had in abundance the one quality the rest of the Wexford team lacked that day: presence. The reticent, awkward teenager transformed into PT Barnum when he put on a pair of football boots. He was born to display his footballing skills in front of an audience and this was the biggest audience he'd ever had.

His first contribution was a sublime piece of skill. He drifted out to the left-wing and instantly trapped a thirty-five-yard pass from Demo Larkin with his left foot. All in one movement, he then slotted it deftly through the legs of the oncoming QPR centre half with his right, shouting *'Nuts!'* as he left the defender in his wake. Another QPR defender arrived on the scene and cleared the ball before Tennant could get to it.

Tennant's cameo lasted no more than five seconds. Nonetheless, it was a bold declaration of intent.

Andy Clarke's eyes narrowed. It was his job to notice such glimpses of raw potential. He intuitively warned the towering centre half who Tennant had just nutmegged:

"Tommy! Stay tight on fourteen."

Tommy wasn't happy. His teammates taunted him with chants of *'nuuuts'* in their best Irish accents. Tommy cursed to himself and resolved to *'let Tennant know he was there'* the next time Tennant got the ball.

Tennant heard Andy Clarke's warning to Tommy and delighted in the attention. He could feel his chest expanding. Like a matador priming a bull, he mischievously stomped on Tommy's foot as they jogged back into position. He then had the temerity to complain to the ref that Tommy had trod on *his* foot. A shouting match ensued between Tennant and Tommy. Both were 'limping'. The ref had to stop the game.

"Any more guff from you two and I'll send you both off."

The game resumed. Tennant blew a kiss at Tommy when the ref wasn't looking. By now Tommy was ready to throttle him.

*****

Tennant didn't have to wait long for his moment of greatness to flicker. Five minutes later Demo Larkin got the ball. He spotted Tennant *'giving him the eyes'* to signal that Tennant wanted the ball down the right-wing, and dinked a lovely ball over the head of the QPR full-back.

Tennant gambled that Demo would pick up his signal. He was already gliding past the full-back down the right-wing when the ball left Demo's boot.

There was still a lot to do. As he approached the ball, Tennant could see in the corner of his eye his favourite QPR defender, Tommy, hurtling towards him, his nostrils flaring, mind filled with bad intentions. He sensed a sliding tackle coming that was intended to put him and the ball well over the side-line and to teach Tennant not to try any funny stuff again.

The double drag-back that Tennant then performed was a skill he learned playing street football on his estate. It was the kind of risky, elaborate skill quickly jettisoned during high-pressure matches in front of keen-eyed scouts and grasping parents. However, unlike the QPR lads, Tennant still played street football. To him, the double drag-back came as naturally as riding a bike. To the rest of us, it was art. Seeing the QPR centre half sliding full speed over the line in Tennant's wake as Tennant now manoeuvred the ball towards the edge of the box was like watching Freddie Mercury perform at *Live Aid*: genius.

The last QPR defender was not going to make the same mistake. Instead, he made a different one.

Assuming Tennant was right footed, like most players, he ushered Tennant over to his right side and Tennant's left. It was like the Red Sea opening for Tennant, who was now only twenty-five yards from goal. Tennant took two touches on his left foot, looked up, spotted that the QPR keeper had encroached well off his line in anticipation of a shot, and then attempted the most audacious lob ever seen on a Wexford pitch.

East End United's ground fell silent as the ball gracefully rotated through the air, beyond the outstretched, flapping gloves of the forlorn retreating QPR keeper. So silent that the owls in the surrounding trees might have heard the sound of Scoop Murphy's notebook falling gently to the turf as he bore witness to the kind of skill that inspires sports journalists to spend their lives eulogising others.

When the ball finally descended and bounced casually into the QPR net, a cacophony of unbridled joy erupted all over the ground:

"YEEEEESSSSS!"
"DEEECCYYYY TENNANT!"
"STICK THAT UP THE QUEEN'S ARSE!"

Clem Roche gazed in deep amaze, speechless.

Chopper Ryan kicked the spare balls on the side-line as high as he could. Parents fist-pumped the air. Young girls did cartwheels. The ref tried not to smile.

It was more than a goal. It was an act of defiance.

Tennant sprinted in celebration towards the corner flag in trademark aeroplane pose. All his teammates, and a few of their younger siblings from the crowd, sprinted after him like fugitives in ecstatic pursuit. After what they had just seen, no one present would have been surprised if they had all taken flight, like ET and the boys on the BMXs. Within seconds, Tennant was engulfed by his pursuers, still wondering if they were dreaming. A human pyramid was formed with Tennant's aeroplane arms just about visible beneath it.

When Tennant eventually got up, he touched the grass again, blessed himself, and saluted the crowd as he jogged back towards the halfway line. It was, as they said, *just like watching Brazil'*.

*****

Clem Roche's competitive instincts kicked in. Wexford were 1–3 down but there were still fifteen minutes left. The game had suddenly become a match. He roared encouragement at each of the Wexford players, hoping to stir something in them that he knew was there.

He needn't have bothered. Tennant's goal was like the first shot of a rebellion and the Wexford lads came from rebel stock. The uprising continued for the remainder of the match with Wexford laying siege to the QPR goal. The emboldened Wexford lads upped their physicality levels considerably. The QPR boys didn't like it. A couple of skirmishes broke out. They quickly developed into melees when the 'peacemakers' from the Wexford team arrived, ostensibly to 'break it up' but really to provoke further confrontation. The QPR lads were quick to complain to the ref. The Wexford lads were well used to fighting and didn't need the ref to protect them. It was *their* pitch. They smelled fear. The crowd on the side-lines were loving it and delighted in throwing petrol on the flames:

"G'wan Browner."
"Rip his head off."

Wexford won a corner with just four minutes left. Tennant ran over to take it. Just before he did, he raised all ten fingers high in the air above his head. It looked like a signal from an elaborate training ground move that Wexford had spent hours rehearsing. It wasn't. However, Tennant had seen his Brazilian idols on the television make similar gestures before taking corners and it looked good.

It worked a treat. Tennant glided a beautiful ball to the back post. Demo Larkin leapt like a salmon above all the QPR defenders to head it back across the goal into the top right corner of the net. 2-3!

The celebrations were more muted this time. Demo Larkin ran to collect the ball from the net and then sprinted back to place it on the centre spot for QPR's kick-off, keen to lose as little time as possible. Clem Roche hurriedly beckoned the lads back into their positions so the match could re-start. There were still three minutes left!

*****

The last chance of the match fell, appropriately, to Tennant. Demo Larkin knocked the ball deep into the QPR half. It fell to Tennant just outside the box.

Fate decreed that it dropped towards his right foot, rather than his preferred left. Tennant's scruffy effort managed to hit the post, accompanied by overly dramatic *'Ooooooooos'* from the Wexford supporters, hoping to somehow will the ball into the net.

Instead, it rebounded out to Tommy, the QPR defender. Knowing the full-time whistle was imminent, he hoofed it as far as he could out of play and into an adjoining farmer's land, so as to wind down the clock.

It was the biggest compliment he could have paid the Wexford lads: QPR had had enough.

*****

Shortly afterwards the full-time whistle blew and the hostilities ceased instantly. The teams shook hands and headed for their Portakabins. The QPR boys were looking forward to getting back on their (locked) bus.

The Wexford Portakabin was a riotous scene of celebration and profanity, engulfed by the rank odour of fresh sweat, stale sweat from odd socks discarded after previous games, and cigarette smoke. Nobody cared. The Wexford team, half naked, and Clem Roche banged their fists on the walls and sang a famous old rebel song as if their lives depended on it:

"Will you stand in the van like a true Irishman?"
"Will you go and fight the forces of the Crown?"
"Will you march with O'Neill through an Irish battlefield?"
"For tonight we're going to free ol' Wexford town."

The QPR players trudging past did not know what to make of it. Maybe you have to be Irish to appreciate glorious defeat.

One of their coaches was unimpressed. He thought the song was provocative.

"Blimey, imagine if they'd <u>actually</u> won the game!" he said, sarcastically, in an accent like something out of East Enders.

His remark drew a loud, pointed laugh from his players.

Scoop Murphy overheard and couldn't resist responding:

"And imagine if your lot had <u>actually</u> won the War of Independence."

*****

Clem Roche was surprised to see Clarke in a huddle with the other QPR mentors when he emerged, still smiling, from the Wexford Portakabin. Clarke had been waiting for Clem Roche and made a beeline for him.

"Thanks again, Clem. That's a spirited bunch of lads you have there."

"No problem, Andy. It was a great experience for our boys and an honour for us all to play with a top team like yours. I hope it was good preparation for the Dublin tournament."

"Absolutely, it was…"

It was a similar conversation to the one they had when the ref blew his whistle at full time. Clem Roche wondered where it was leading. Clarke paused for a moment and then got to the point:

"Tell me, Clem, why didn't you play number fourteen from the start? He was bloody lively when he came on."

Clem Roche was an honest, church-going man. He knew well where the conversation was leading and did what any good man would do in the circumstances: he lied.

"He is just back from an Achilles injury. I couldn't chance him from the start as he has been injured for a long time and I promised his club I would only give him twenty minutes or so. It was a shame as it might have been a different match if I could have started with him."
"Do you think he would come over to us for a trial?"
"I'll ask him."
"What about his parents?"
"His parents…"

Clem Roche paused for a moment, looking around to see if Josie was there.

"They won't mind," he said solemnly, realising she wasn't.

*****

An hour later, the double doors of the Oulart Tavern swung violently open as a neighbour of Josie's thundered into the lounge. He spotted Josie nursing a whiskey at the bar.

"Well now, Josie Tennant, do you want the good news or the bad news?" he asked, mischievously.

"Wha...?"
Josie was half cut after a few hours on her stool.

"Well, the bad news is that you've scrounged your last free drink in here. The drinks will be on you from now on, my lassie..."

"But the good news is that Deccy scored the goal of the season against QPR and they've offered him a trial! Deccy's one-step away from becoming a professional footballer in England! He was the 'man of the match'. They carried him off the pitch shoulder high. He has a trial with Queens Park Rangers, woman! You may start packing your bags for London."

Shame sobered Josie up instantly.

"Are you jokin' me?" she said.
"It's as true as I'm standing her in front of you. You should have seen him. He was unbelievable. You can ask anyone on Main Street. The whole town's talking about it."

That was the moment that Josie realised she would never forgive herself for missing the match.

She left her half-drunk whiskey, pulled up the hood of her tracksuit top, and walked out into the evening air.

*****

Tennant was the first player from Wexford to get a trial with a professional team. It would take place in QPR's training ground in London, three weeks later.

Wexford's gallant effort, triggered by Tennant's wonder-goal, dominated the sports pages of the *Wexford Times* and echoed around the narrow streets of the town. Scoop Murphy's impartial match report, headlined *'Wexford Youths terrorise QPR'* adorned classrooms across the county. By the time it hit the printing press, Tennant had beaten *'at least four'* QPR defenders before executing his storied lob from *'all of thirty-five yards'*. It was remarkable how incidental the score line seemed to the wonder of it all.

Tennant became a transient celebrity as news of his QPR trial spread. Mooney's' stores, the largest and oldest shop on Main Street, sponsored him with a new tracksuit, shin pads, and boots for the trip. Girls giggled nervously as he passed. The patrons in the Oulart Tavern drank deep and spoke in hushed tones of how much money his first contract might be worth.

Tennant himself wasn't too bothered that Josie didn't turn up for the QPR match. However, every well-meaning mention of the match to her only exacerbated her self-loathing. She barely left the house. Tennant was oddly indifferent to all the hullabaloo about his trial. He was worried about leaving his mother alone, even for a few days.

The *Wexford Times* did a short preview of Tennant's trip to QPR. A photographer went to their house for a picture to go with the preview. After a few shots of Tennant posing in his new tracksuit, the photographer remarked:

"We have to get a photo of Wexford's newest superstar with his proud mother too."

He knew the readers would like that and beckoned Josie out to her overgrown back garden where he was taking the shots.

Josie was a reluctant subject. The last thing she wanted was to be in the paper and she was still unsure of where she stood with Tennant. She shuffled uneasily to within a few feet of her boy, looking like she wanted the ground to swallow her. Tennant, sensing her unease, moved across to her and put his arm around her soft waist with a broad smile. She was still his ma.

"Will this do?"

Josie extended one arm tentatively around Tennant, wiped away tears with the other, and tried to smile.

*****

Later that evening, Josie telephoned Clem Roche, drunk, and asked him if he would go to London with Tennant instead of her.

"Sure, I wouldn't be of any use over there," she said.

She was right.

Clem Roche paused. Just hearing the word 'London' evoked painful memories of Harley Street. He sighed silently, then agreed without question, and made arrangements with QPR.

*****

At six-thirty the next morning Tennant's doorbell rang, several times. Eventually, Tennant appeared, half-asleep, in football shorts, a dressing gown and flip-flops.

"Clem? What are you doing here? What time is it?"

"Time to get fit. Hop in," he said, pointing to his car.

Before Tennant knew it, he was on his way to begin a three-week boot camp for the QPR trial.

"Where are we heading?" he asked.

"Curracloe," said Clem Roche.

Curracloe beach has mile after mile of soft, golden sand at the foot of tall dunes overlooking the Irish Sea. It was then known locally as 'Ireland's best-kept secret'. In the pre-internet age, it had somehow managed to largely escape the attention of tourists. The people of Wexford were glad to have it unspoiled, all to themselves. It was a great place to clear your head. Just gazing out over the sea from the dunes could soothe even the most troubled mind.

Tennant was not there to be soothed. Clem Roche had devised a training schedule for him that would push him to his limits. He could not teach Tennant any new skills in just three weeks but he could surely improve his fitness.

*****

'Where are the balls, Clem?' Tennant asked on arrival.

'At home,' Clem responded, ominously.

Clem Roche's primitive workout routine for Tennant consisted of Tennant sprinting up the dunes and walking back down, with some press-ups thrown in for good measure when Tennant couldn't run anymore.

The first morning was hell. After six sprints Tennant doubled over and vomited up last night's takeaway.

'I can't do this, Clem,' he said, gasping for air and deeply regretting his late-night cigarette the previous evening.

'Of course, you can. Take a quick breather.'

'I can't catch my breath, Clem…' said Tennant, his voice quivering.

Clem Roche paused, seeing that both Tennant's body and spirit were breaking.

'I'll tell you what. I'll do the sprints with you. Sure, if an old man can do them, then so can you.'

Clem Roche gave Tennant five minutes to recover. They completed the remaining dune sprints together.

Early morning walkers watched with bemusement for the next three weeks as Tennant and his middle-aged coach scattered seagulls zigzagging up the dunes. Clem Roche had water and fruit for them at the end of each session. Never a man for the healthy option, Tennant usually passed on the fruit but the water was the best thing he had ever tasted. He gulped it down. They both enjoyed the post-work-out chat on the top of the dunes.

Clem Roche took satisfaction from seeing Tennant progress, albeit from a very low base. He was proud of the commitment the lad had shown. However, setting off on his post-round after their final session, his abiding sense was that they needed another four or five weeks' work for his protégé to be ready for what he was about to face.

*****

On 7 July 1988, Clem Roche and Tennant got the ferry from Rosslare to Fishguard. From there they caught a bus to London, where they were warmly greeted after their long journey by Andy Clarke.

Clarke gave them a brief tour of QPR's training ground. Tennant and Clem Roche were awestruck. There were football pitches as far as the eye could see. The manicured lawns that QPR's academy used as training pitches were as smooth as putting greens, complete with sprinkler systems. The clubhouse had changing rooms bigger than Tennant's house, a gymnasium, a massage room, a swimming pool, a player's lounge and a restaurant serving nutritious meals. It was a long way from East End United's stinking Portakabins.

Clarke explained that Tennant would play two trial matches, one on each of the following days. He told Tennant that he was really looking forward to seeing Tennant play and encouraged him to express himself as best he could. He then arranged a taxi to their hotel and wished them both a good night's sleep ahead of Tennant's first trial match the next day.

QPR had paid for a nice hotel for two nights. Tennant and Clem Roche had a quiet dinner together and, sensing the task ahead, agreed that an early night was a good idea. However, Tennant's sense of novelty from staying in a hotel room was quickly replaced by one of unease. Alone with his thoughts, he played his trial match in his head a hundred times over. The harder he tried to sleep the more it evaded him.

Tennant felt as if he hadn't slept a wink when Clem Roche knocked on his door at 7am the following morning.

*****

The trial began at 9 am. Tennant spent the first hour being assessed by QPR's physical therapy team in the gymnasium. Every muscle in his body was stretched and manoeuvred as they quietly marvelled at Tennant's inflexibility and ungainly posture, all under the watchful eye of Andy Clarke.

After a short break, a QPR fitness coach was dispatched by the physical therapy team to assess Tennant's cardiovascular fitness. He was six-foot two inches of pure muscle and looked like a drill sergeant from the SAS. Tennant and Clem Roche were chatting outside the clubhouse when he jogged briskly around the corner towards them with a clipboard under one arm.

"You must be Declan Tennant," he said, assertively extending his hand for a manly handshake.

"Yeah," said Tennant, feeling the force of his grip.

"Are you ready for your fitness test?" He said, grinning, with the look of a man who knew well the answer was an emphatic 'no'.

The only 'fitness test' Tennant had ever done was sprinting up the dunes in Curracloe. He had a feeling he would not enjoy this.

"Alright…" Tennant responded, hesitantly.

Two plastic cones were placed twenty-metres apart. Tennant had to run from one cone to another in-between 'bleeps' played on a tape recorder. As the test progressed, the time that elapsed between the bleeps reduced, increasing Tennant's required speed. The purpose of the test was to see how long Tennant could keep getting from one cone to another before the tape bleeped. Level ten to fourteen was average for Tennant's age group in the QPR academy, with the more athletic boys reaching nineteen or twenty. Tennant's lungs were on fire by the time his body gave up at level five, wheezing and coughing.

Andy Clarke and the fitness coach withdrew a few paces to assess the morning's results. Clem Roche noticed the fitness coach raising his eyebrows and shaking his head. Clarke looked chastened by the conversation. He had arrived back from Ireland with rave reports on a young lad who he claimed might just be *'something special'*. Now the Special One was doubled over, hocking up tar-coloured phlegm like a geriatric smoker awaiting a lung transplant.

Clem Roche was concerned that this might be the end of the trial before Tennant had even kicked a ball. Desperate, he tentatively approached Clarke when the fitness coach departed:

'Andy, do you have a minute?'
'What is it, Clem?' Clarke said, abruptly.

Clem Roche was a little taken aback by Clarke's brusque response.

"Look Andy, I know he is not in the best of shape at the moment but the season is over back home so he has not had a match since we played your lads."

"I see, Clem. Thanks. But there was something else from this morning's assessment that is puzzling us."

"What's that?" said Clem Roche, worried.

"Our physical therapy team could find no trace of the Achilles injury you mentioned in Wexford. No swelling. No stiffness. No scar tissue. Nothing. It was as if it never happened. He may be unfit but he's the fastest healer we've ever seen..."

Clem Roche was dumbstruck. Lying was foreign to him but he had not been caught lying since he was a schoolboy.

"Make sure he is here for a match at 11:30. Kick-off is at 12," said Clarke, walking away.

Clem Roche was shaken by the exchange. However, his resolve returned when he saw the concerned look on Tennant's face, who had been observing his conversation with Clarke.

"What did he say, Clem?"

"Don't worry, Deccy. You're here to play football, not run marathons. We have to be back here at 11:30 for a match."

*****

Later that morning Tennant was picked to line up for a QPR academy team in a match against Oxford United's academy. Clem Roche waited outside as Tennant brought his Oulart United gear bag into the changing rooms.

Andy Clarke gave Tennant his QPR kit and showed him where to get changed. There were brief pleasantries from a couple of QPR academy players who recognised Tennant but nothing more. Trialists came and went regularly. No one paid much attention to them unless they stayed around.

Tennant had never been in a dressing room like it. There were a mix of accents and races from all over Britain and beyond. The QPR players had made good use of the gym. A few were built like Arnold Schwarzenegger. The noise was oppressive. Some players exchanged loud, nervous banter with each other across the room. Others danced and sang along to high tempo pop songs which Tennant did not recognise blaring out of a ghetto blaster. The smell of whatever balm the QPR players were rubbing into their muscular legs was overpowering.

Tennant felt like an imposter, sitting in the corner, shrinking. Then Andy Clarke came in and everything stopped. He turned over a whiteboard and began using a black marker to give instructions to each player on match tactics. Tennant nodded when Clarke told him something about *'running the channels'* but Clarke may as well have been speaking a different language.

Tennant put on his QPR kit and was walking out towards the pitch when another QPR coach stopped him.

"You can't wear those boots out there, son. They'll be like stilts. Put on mouldies."

'Mouldies' are football boots with short, moulded plastic studs. They are perfect for a hard pitch with short grass on a sunny day. The football season in Wexford ran from

September to May when the turf was damp. Everyone wore long, metal studs. Tennant did not have mouldies.

The QPR coach was right; Tennant would have turned his ankle in long metal studs. Embarrassingly, he had no option but to wear the white Adidas trainers he had worn to the ground. Tennant's trial occurred in the era before image rights and boot deals. He was the only player not wearing black boots. He looked and felt like an amateur surrounded by professionals.

The other QPR striker approached Tennant just before kick-off.

"What's your name, mate?"

Tennant was not sure what to say. He was 'Deccy' to his friends but 'Declan' to others.

"Declan," he said hesitantly.

The whistle blew a second later before he could ask his teammate's name. Game on.

The first half passed in a blur. Oxford United were on top. Little ball made its way to Tennant who was unusually passive. His control was fine on the rare occasions when he got the ball but he was not on the same wavelength as his teammates. His passes went astray, his impact minimal.

He was not required for the second half. He changed on his own in the dressing room as his teammates returned to the pitch.

He and Clem Roche returned to their hotel, dejected.

*****

After a couple of hours ruminating on their beds, Clem Roche suddenly knocked on his door.

"Deccy, I've got a plan. Get up."

His plan involved retail therapy in London. JD Sports on Oxford Street described itself as *'the home of football'*. It had 'home' and 'away' football kits for clubs Tennant had never even heard of. However, it was boots he and Clem Roche were after. After forty-five minutes tormenting the assistant on the differences between various brands, Tennant finally settled on the boots he wanted, complete with mouldies.

"You can save your trainers for Wimbledon now, Deccy," Clem Roche said, jokingly, as he handed Tennant the new boots at the till.

It was a nice end to a tough day.

The word 'thanks' did not seem sufficient to Tennant to express his gratitude to Clem Roche for the boots, for everything. No one except Josie had ever done so much for him. Frustratingly, in that instant, he could not think of what else to say. So he just said it twice.

"Thanks, Clem. Thank you."

He need not have worried. Tennant's bashful glow told Clem Roche all he needed to know. It did Clem Roche's heart good.

"I guess that's what it's like to have a da," Tennant thought to himself.

"I guess that's what it's like to have a son," Clem Roche thought to himself.

Tennant spent the evening breaking in the leather of his new boots on the corridors of their hotel. He was still nervous but at least he knew now what was ahead of him.

*****

There were no physical assessments or fitness tests the next morning. This time Tennant was a substitute in another match for a slightly younger QPR academy team against Charlton Athletic's academy.

Clem Roche's heart sank when he learned that Tennant was not starting the game. He knew that when a trialist is relegated to the substitutes' bench that means that the trial club has seen enough. Nonetheless, he resolved to keep his emotions to himself. He chatted cheerfully to Tennant as the matched progressed, telling Tennant that he was *'just as good'* as one of the QPR strikers who has having a frustrating match.

With thirty minutes left, Clarke gave Tennant the signal that he would be coming on shortly. Clem Roche beckoned Tennant over as he warmed up:

"No whatever you do out there today, Deccy, I want you to enjoy yourself, right?" he said, with the air of a prison warden delivering a condemned inmate's final meal.

Tennant nodded and readied himself to enter the fray. He also knew that he wasn't coming back to QPR.

A second substitute striker was coming on the same time. He stood beside Tennant as they waited for the linesman to catch the referee's attention. At six feet three inches tall, and every inch of it muscle, complete with dreadlocks tied back in a ponytail, he looked more like a rugby player than a footballer.

"Wesley Ferdinand," he said slowly, politely extending his hand to Tennant. *"Call me Weso."*

"Declan Tennant." said Tennant, firmly shaking his hand. *"Call me Deccy."*

And on they went.

Tennant made a better impression during his half-hour cameo. Ferdinand was the perfect partner for him. It took two of Charlton Athletic's defenders to deal with his bustling presence, allowing Tennant more time on the ball. Tennant had some typically deft touches and even a trademark left-footed pile driver at goal from fully thirty yards which whistled an inch wide of the post.

"Good effort, man," said Ferdinand, with a thumbs up, in a Caribbean accent.

"Cheers, Weso," said Tennant in his thick Wexford accent, reciprocating the thumbs up gesture.

Clem Roche smiled at the blossoming of an unlikely partnership between the scrawny Wexford teenager and his muscular Trinidadian teammate.

Tennant was not the best player on the pitch but this time he made his mark. He got to finish the match, shake the opposition's hands and chat briefly to his new pal, Weso, in the dressing room afterwards. He knew that he had contributed something to the game. Even Andy Clarke seemed relieved that Tennant had shown glimpses of what he had raved to his QPR colleagues about.

*****

Clarke approached Clem Roche while Tennant was getting changed:

"I'm glad he got to show us a little of himself out there today, Clem. The boy has a lot of talent. If I'd spotted him three or four years ago then we might have a professional footballer on our hands today. However, under League rules, we have to either offer the boys a contract or let them go when they turn seventeen. Unfortunately, there's just too much work to be done with Deccy and not enough time to do it. I'm sorry but I hope he continues to enjoy his football at home. Hopefully, he will remember his performance today when he wears this," he said, handing Clem Roche a package.

It was a bag from the QPR club shop containing a QPR tracksuit, the same shiny blue and white one their team had worn in Wexford.

"I understand, Andy. Thanks for having us," said Clem Roche, earnestly shaking Clarke's hand.

*****

When Tennant emerged from the dressing room he spotted Clem Roche gazing miles out past the QPR pitches.

"Well, Clem."

Clem Roche steadied himself and took a breath.

"Deccy, Andy Clarke was just talking to me and…"

"It's alright, Clem. Sure I'm a Liverpool fan anyway. I could never play for this lot," interrupted Tennant, reading

54

Clem Roche's face and eager to spare him the discomfort of delivering the bad news. It was disappointing but unsurprising.

Clem Roche half-smiled, patted Tennant on the back, gave him the tracksuit, and they left for their hotel.

It was time to go home.

*****

The journey back felt longer than the outbound trip. Tennant was anxious to see Josie. He had no sense of regret as he watched the Welsh coast disappearing into the distance from the ferry deck. He was glad to be going home and maybe that was partly why he was. Accidentally or not, he left his QPR tracksuit on the ferry.

No fanfare greeted Tennant's arrival to an empty house. Later, when asked how it went, he said little more than:

"Alright, I suppose. Played a couple of matches for them."

It soon became apparent that it would not be the manicured pitches of the English First Division but the less illustrious surroundings of the Wexford League that Tennant's skills would adorn for the remainder of his footballing days. Neither Clem Roche nor Tennant said much, other than to confirm that it didn't work out.

The information vacuum about *'what really happened'* was quickly filled by rumour and innuendo. The most prevalent theories ranged from:

"I heard they sent him home after half a match," to

55

"I heard he got homesick and made Clem take him home," to

"His head got too big after he scored that goal against QPR."

A more benign version of events was proffered in the Oulart Tavern:

'They offered him a contract and he told them to stick it where the sun don't shine. Sure, who would look after Josie?'

To me, they had all missed the point. Tennant's unsuccessful trial did not render him a failure any more than the United Irishmen's defeat in 1798 had rendered their rebellion a failure. Defeat and failure are not the same. Whatever happened during his trial, Tennant's performance against QPR had validated Wexford football. We knew after the QPR match that we played in a quality league. Our coaches agreed that their protégés were not far behind the QPR players and therefore they *'must have been doing something right'*. Anyone approaching Tennant's standard could be regarded as *'good enough to get a trial in England'*. A wonder goal scored on a Wexford pitch was every bit as much of a screamer as the same strike watched on *Match of the Day*. Yet that debt which we all owed Tennant was never acknowledged or perhaps even appreciated.

*****

Two years later, our time in St Enda's was over. I headed to university to collect my degree. Tennant headed to Anne Street to collect the dole.

He kept turning out for Oulart United for a few more years. Now, however, the tyranny of expectation weighed heavily on him. I heard in dispatches of occasional flickers of genius. However, those moments no longer hinted at a bright future but instead served as reminders of what might have been. His *'legendary'* status was forever secure in Oulart. However, elsewhere in the county, he had become synonymous with the word *'waster'*.

He was glad to have the excuse of coaching his son's under-six team to justify his decision to hang up his boots when he was just twenty-four.

Clem Roche was sad but unsurprised when word reached him of Tennant's retirement from football. They had lost touch in the intervening years. However, on the rare occasions when their paths crossed, they still joked fondly of their nightmares about ascending the Curracloe dunes together.

*****

Josie passed away soon after. She was sixty-six. The birth of her grandson had given her a new lease of life. However, her years in the jar meant she was a heart attack waiting to happen. Eventually, it did. It was her life's great tragedy that she was somehow incapable of showing herself the same kindness she had so readily shown her son.

She was buried in Crosstown cemetery. Tennant and his young son were the chief mourners, awkward in ill-fitting suits.

I passed her grave once when visiting a relative's. On it was a simple inscription, a fresh wreath, and a red Malahide Steamer glued to the base.

*****

Many years later, I was on a rare visit home to Wexford. My wife offered to cook a family meal. I waited in our car with my 12-year-old son on Main Street as she purchased some final ingredients.

Thursday was dole day and there was a buzz in the town. A drunk figure emerged from a pub doorway across the street, lit a cigarette, and exhaled slowly. It was Tennant. He was barely recognisable. His unruly fringe had been replaced by a receding hairline. His protruding gut dripped out over the waistband in his tracksuit bottoms. He looked like a man who had not kicked a ball in a long time.

The sight of him awoke something in me. I instinctively gave him a nervous wave, forgetting the time that had elapsed. He squinted for a moment, trying to figure out who I was. Then he paused for a few seconds, smiled at me, and put his arms out to make the same aeroplane gesture that I had given him outside the principal's office many years previously.

A drinking buddy appeared with a fag in one hand and a betting slip in the other. They shuffled into the bookmakers next door, deep in animated conversation about the next dead cert.

"Who was that Dad?" my son asked.
"That was Deccy Tennant," I said wistfully.
"Who's Deccy Tennant?"

"The best footballer I've ever seen in the flesh."

"Him? Really? Who did he play for?"

"Oulart United, Wexford Youths, and QPR."

"QPR? In England? No way! For how long?"

"Not long. They offered him a contract but he told them to shove it where the sun don't shine."

THE END